LITTLE GREY RABBIT STORYBOOKS

THE GREAT ADVENTURE
OF HARE

The Great Adventure of Hare
first published in Great Britain in 1931 by
William Heinemann Limited

This edition first published in Great Britain in 1986 by

Octopus Books Limited
59 Grosvenor Street
London W1

© Text Trustees of Alison Uttley Literary Property Trust 1984

This arrangement © 1986 Octopus Books Limited

ISBN 0 7064 2603 7

Produced by
Mandarin Publishers Limited
22a Westlands Road
Quarry Bay, Hong Kong

Printed in Hong Kong

LITTLE GREY RABBIT STORYBOOKS

THE GREAT ADVENTURE
OF HARE

BY ALISON UTTLEY
ILLUSTRATIONS BY MARGARET TEMPEST

OCTOPUS BOOKS LIMITED

It was a lovely midsummer morning, and Hare looked out of his bedroom window on to the fields where cloud shadows were running races. Gentle blue butterflies and fierce little wasps flew among the flowers in the garden below. Hare stroked his whiskers and said 'Just the day for my adventure.'

'Grey Rabbit, Grey Rabbit, come here,' he called over the banisters, 'and bring my walking-stick, will you?'

A scamper of little feet echoed on the brick floor in the kitchen, and Grey Rabbit ran upstairs with a cherry-wood stick and a teazle brush. Hare took down his new blue coat from the hook behind the bedroom door. He put it on, with Grey Rabbit's help, twisting his head to get a good view of the two brass buttons at the back.

G rey Rabbit brushed off some tiny specks of whitewash with her teazle. She had to stand on tip-toes to reach his shoulders, she was so small.

'Are my buttons all right?' asked Hare.

'Yes, like two looking-glasses,' replied Grey Rabbit, as she gave each one a rub with a duster, and then peeped at her face in the dazzling buttons.

'Don't forget your watch,' she added, as the Hare started downstairs.

'Oh dear, how careless you are, Grey Rabbit,' said the Hare, taking a large flat silver watch from the chest of drawers, and putting it in his waistcoat pocket. 'I nearly went without it.'

'It's late,' he continued, 'half-past twelve.'

'Half-past seven by the sun,' said Grey Rabbit, quietly.

'The sun's five hours slow,' returned Hare, as he walked downstairs, and Grey Rabbit stopped behind to hang up his old blue coat, which lay crumpled on the floor.

'Good-bye, Squirrel,' called Hare, as Squirrel looked up from the mittens she was knitting. 'Good-bye, I'm off on my great journey. Good-bye, Grey Rabbit, I shall be back for supper, and mind there is something nice.'

He stepped out of the little door into the sunshine.

'Take care of yourself,' cried Grey Rabbit, running after him and waving her paw. 'Mind the traffic, and give Toad our present.'

'Don't forget to bring a present back,' called Squirrel.

I will bring presents for all three of us,' replied Hare, importantly, as he marched down the garden path, with his head in the air, and his buttons flashing.

He was going to visit the famous Toad who lived in the Ash Wood, at the other side of the wide valley. Squirrel had laughed when he said he was going, and said, 'You never dare.'

'Darsen't I?' he replied. 'You'll see!'

Grey Rabbit had looked a little anxious, but she was pleased that the timid Hare was so bold.

She decided to give the house a summer-cleaning whilst he was away. So Squirrel took her knitting up an apple-tree to be out of the way, and Little Grey Rabbit, with scrubbing brush and pail, prepared to clean the rooms.

Hare shut the garden gate with a bang, and

flicked his handkerchief at three flies who seemed determined to travel with him. He picked a sprig of sweet marjoram from the bush outside the gate, put it in his buttonhole, and prepared to leap over the brook.

But he changed his mind, and sat down by the water, turning this way and that to see his buttons. As he twisted and craned his neck, a mocking voice cried, 'Haven't you gone yet? You'll never get to Ash Wood if you don't start,' and he saw Squirrel's face peering down from the apple-tree.

Hare sprang up and marched off pretending not to hear. He entered the big wood where Wise Owl lived.

All was quiet there, and the flies deserted him to find another traveller going some happier way. He held his stick firmly and whistled softly as he walked warily, fearfully, on the soft moss. His eyes looked at each side, and his ears, pricked back, kept guard behind. He was so intent on this sideways and backward glance that he did not see where he was going, and suddenly he bumped into a scared rabbit, who also was looking behind him.

With cries of alarm they both fell head over heels. The rabbit picked himself up, muttering, 'Silly old Clumsy,' and ran on. Hare brushed his coat, and picked off some old leaves which clung to it. He examined his watch, and searched for his stick which had fallen into a blackberry bush.

A sound came from behind a tree, and a Cock Pheasant walked out with proudly lifted legs.

'Good morning, Pheasant,' said the Hare. 'It's a fine day today. I've just had a tumble— some stupid rabbit, not looking where he was going.'

'Hush,' whispered the Pheasant. 'Don't talk so loudly, young fellow.'

'Why, what's the matter? Don't you live here?' asked Hare.

'No, my home is in the glade yonder,' said the Pheasant, pointing with one foot to a clearing which showed light among the dense trees, 'but I don't want these fellows to know. Too many shady people in this wood. Break open a house, rob, no respect for property.

'Only last week I had my water-butt emptied and my larder ransacked by a thief.'

'Who was it, do you think?' asked Hare.

'It was Jay; he left a bit of his blue scarf behind him.'

'He daren't come to our house,' said Hare.

'You never know. There are other robbers besides Jay. Don't boast till you are out of the wood;' and saying this, the Pheasant flew away with a heavy flap of his wings.

Hare ran on until he came to a great oak tree with a little door, and a silver bell hanging by a thin rope.

'Should I? Should I? Should I ring Moldy Warp's bell?' thought he. 'Suppose Owl should come. What could I say? I'll ask the way to Ash Wood.'

He pulled the string, and 'Tinkle, tinkle,' sang the tiny bell. Hare got ready to run, but a sleepy voice called, 'What do you want, Hare?' and Owl looked out, blinking in the sunlight.

Hare faltered, 'Er—er—er—which way is the way to Ash Wood, please, Wise Owl?'

The Owl looked down severely, and Hare quickly got out his silk handkerchief from his coat pocket and waved it violently.

'What do you mean by waking me up for such a question? Where is your money?'

Hare started, remembering how little Grey Rabbit had lost her tail; but Owl had seen the shining buttons.

'I'll take those buttons from the back of your coat,' said he, and he clambered down, and cut them off before Hare could say 'Jigger-jagger.'

'Go through the wood, cross the Teazle field, turn to the right through the village, to the left across the railway line, up the fields, through Bilberry Wood, past Home Farm, and the Ash Wood is at the top of the hill,' said the Owl, all in one breath.

'Thank you,' muttered Hare, retreating.

'A Fox lives in Bilberry Wood,' called Wise Owl, and Hare turned pale. 'I think I shall go home,' said he.

Owl had already climbed upstairs again, and shut the door. He took some sealing wax and stuck the buttons on his night-cap, before he went to sleep.

Overhead a loud screaming laugh startled Hare, who stood undecided and alarmed. A blue Jay, who had been listening, flew by.

'Ha ha! ha ha! Frightened Hare! Timid Hare!' he mocked.

Hare grabbed his stick, straightened his shoulders, and began to whistle, 'Rule, Britannia,' which annoyed the Jay, and off he went.

'I expect the Fox won't notice me. I'm a pretty fast runner,' said he.

He ran through the seeding blue-bells, and purple foxgloves, flowering under the nut trees and great oaks. He ran down the stony path, where ants laboured among the patches of yellow pimpernel, under the roof of beech and elm, to the gate at the end of the wood.

In the Teazle field were red butterflies with

their little baskets, gathering honey from the ragwort, brown bumble bees, eager to talk to anyone, busy hoverflies, with no time to spare, red-caped ladybirds, and field mice in bonnets and shawls, running on errands, strolling home, gossiping by the tiny green paths, playing on swings and roundabouts, chattering and singing. It was such a busy world after the quiet wood. Hare walked across the field swinging his stick, feeling very important in his bright coat among all these little people. He nodded to strangers and talked to acquaintances.

What nice fellows these were! They all knew Little Grey Rabbit, for she got her teazle brushes here, and Hare answered many kind inquiries about her.

Where are you going, stranger?' asked a Brown Rabbit.

'To Ash Wood, to visit Toad,' answered Hare, pompously.

'My! You are a traveller!' exclaimed the Rabbit, admiringly.

'I am that,' said Hare, who seldom went beyond the garden gate.

'What other countries have you seen?' inquired the Rabbit, and three others came close to listen.

'Well—er—I've seen too many to tell you about today. I am a very famous Hare.'

They pressed closer and stared at him with wide, innocent eyes.

'I'm so famous,' continued Hare, 'that I'm called—or to be exact, I shall be called, after this journey—"Columbus Hare".'

That's a travelling name. Columbus was a Hare who crossed rivers, and fields, and woods, till he found another country where black rabbits lived.'

'Will you tell us about Ash Wood and Toad when you come back, Columbus Hare?'

'That I will, and I'll bring you a piece of grey ashen wood, to show I've been there, if you meet me at'—here he consulted his watch—'at half-past twelve.'

'There's a Fox in Bilberry Wood, I've been told by my wife's brother,' said a quiet little Hedgehog who had come up.

'I'm not afraid of a Fox,' cried Hare, boldly, and he threw his stick up in the air and caught it.

The Rabbits gazed admiringly at him.

'Is that a magic on your chain?' asked a very

small Rabbit timidly, stretching up a paw to the watch.

'Yes, it's a great magic. It's better than the sun,' said Hare.

He sat on a stone by the clear tinkling spring which jutted out of the earth like a baby fountain, and ran down the sloping field among pink centaury and short green reeds. The rabbits and the Hedgehog sat by him, and two water wagtails, chattering and merry, joined the company.

Hare picked a bunch of reeds and wove a green basket for the wagtails. The Hedgehog dabbled in the spring with his little hands, and the Rabbits played 'Here we go round the blackberry-bush'.

Then Hare got out his sandwiches and divided them among his new friends, who were proud to sit down with such a bold adventurer.

After they had eaten even the lettuce leaves in which the food was wrapped, Hare sent them away. He curled himself up in a patch of warm long grass in the middle of the bushes, he put his two paws under his nose, and fell asleep.

He was awakened by the youngest Rabbit who tugged at his watch. Hare sprang up in a hurry; he had slept longer than he intended.

'Be off, you naughty child,' he scolded, and she scuttled home to her mother.

He left the field by a gap in the hedge, crossed the dusty lane, and ran along the narrow road through the village.

A tortoiseshell cat arched her back and spat at him, and a dog barked and tugged at his chain. A baby opened his eyes very wide, and pointed at him, and an old man fumbled in his pocket for his spectacles to stare at him.

He leapt the limestone wall, and crossed the field to the railway. The gleaming hot rails burnt his toes, and the roar of a distant train terrified him, as he scampered across and hid in the grass at the other side whilst the express rushed by.

'That's a Dragon,' said he, mopping his head. 'I must be in China. I *shall* have some adventures to talk about when I get home.'

He climbed up a steep path into a rocky wood, 'on the edge of the world,' thought he.

Great cool spaces were about him, and a

green roof above, held up by trees like pillars. The softest moss covered the rocks lying about on the ground, and bilberry bushes, jewelled with pink flowers, grew by the path. The sun shone through the lacy boughs and dappled his fur and blue coat with yellow circles. The air was so cold and fresh, like a drink of spring water.

'Can you tell me the time?' asked a silken voice, and Hare saw a fine gentleman in a red coat sitting on a fallen tree.

'Half-past twelve,' said Hare, consulting his watch.

'Really? As early as that? Will you do me the favour of joining me in a bottle of cherry brandy?' asked the polite gentleman, and he brought out a bottle from his pocket.

T hank you,' said Hare, regretfully, 'I am late for an appointment, but I shall be glad to join you on my way back.'

'I will wait here for you,' said the gentleman in red, smiling at Hare, 'and perhaps you would like to see my collection of birds' eggs?'

'Delighted,' said Hare, who was flattered by this notice.

'I am a bit of a collector myself. I collect Noughts and Crosses. I won't forget,' and he trotted on, whilst the fine gentleman gazed longingly after him.

There was a curious smell which disturbed Hare. It wasn't mignonette, or lavender, or sausages, or fried eggs. 'It must be some foreign scent on his handkerchief,' thought Hare.

He picked a branch of honeysuckle and twined it round his head, and held his sprig of marjoram to his nose, but the smell remained until he left the wood and crossed the fields to the stone farm on the high ridge.

Dappled cows stood under the trees, swishing their tails as they waited to be milked. Two great mares rubbed noses as they talked about their foals, and a score of hens chattered excitedly about the Fox, who, the night before, had tried to open the hen-house door. Hare loped by without speaking, he was an outsider in this intimate company.

In front of him lay Ash Wood, with its grey trees and rustling leaves.

Apple-green moths and honey-bees came to meet him as he entered. The flowers grew in groups, a patch of red campion here, a clump of forget-me-nots there, bugle, ground-ivy, and tall bell-flowers, in their blues and purples, like mists on the ground.

'Herbs for old Toad, I suppose,' said Hare to himself, as he looked round. 'He does a lot of doctoring, they say.'

In the middle of the wood was a bog, fragrant with many coloured orchis, and there, perched on an island, was a small house with a roof thatched with rushes. Over it hung a willow, and round it, half concealing the roof, were bushes of bog-myrtle.

'Who's there?' boomed a voice, as Hare waded through the bog with his coat-tails turned up.

'It's Hare, from Grey Rabbit's house, over the valley,' said Hare.

The little door opened slowly and an immense Toad waddled out, leaning on a crutch. His eyes were bright as green lamps, and his cheeks were wrinkled with age.

He wore a green coat and yellow breeches, old and creased, but Hare felt a shabby nobody when he looked at the wise animal.

'I have brought a present,' said Hare, as the Toad gazed at him without speaking.

He searched all his pockets, dipping into one side and then the other. He hunted and hunted, and then took off his coat. He looked in his waistcoat pockets, but it wasn't there.

The Toad stood, still leaning on his crutch, whilst the flustered Hare turned everything inside out.

'Here it is,' he cried at last. 'Grey Rabbit

stitched it inside my coat-lining lest I should lose it on the way.' He cut the stitches and brought out an egg-beater.

'It's to beat eggs, whip them, you know, make them frothy,' explained Hare breathlessly. 'We thought it would be useful.'

Toad was entranced. For all his learning he had seen nothing like it. He held it between his knees and turned the handle so that the wheels whizzed. Then he held it in the bog so that the water frothed and foamed. He took up a handful and sipped it. 'Lemonade,' said he.

He whizzed it in a bowl of cream which stood on the door-step. The cream foamed in a whiteness.

'Butter,' said he.

'Come in, come in, Hare,' he cried, throwing open the little door; and, stooping very low, Hare entered the cool-flagged hall and walked through to a courtyard, where a fountain played.

Toad beat up the fountain and made rainbows of light.

Then he rang a hare-bell, and two frogs appeared.

'Bring refreshments for this gentleman,' he commanded, 'and a bowl of wood-pigeons' eggs.'

The two frogs returned with red wine and saffron cake which Hare ate greedily. The Toad beat up the eggs, mixed them with the wine, and made wonderful drinks which astonished Hare.

'I have no teeth,' he explained. 'It's a most useful gift, most useful. I have never been so pleased.'

He took Hare to a cupboard which was crammed with odds and ends picked up in the woods. There were skipping ropes, shuttle-cocks, rings and pebbles, tin cans and ginger-beer bottles, kettles, mouth-organs, matches—all the things that picnickers had left behind.

'Choose a present for yourself, and one for each of your friends,' said Toad, and Hare hunted among the medley to find something suitable.

He chose a tiny pair of slippers made from the bark of the silver birch, which some rabbit had lost, for Little Grey Rabbit, and a boxwood flute which a blackbird had dropped, for Squirrel, and a penknife with a corkscrew for himself.

Then Toad unlocked a secret drawer and took

out a small green bottle labelled VENOM.

'I shall give you a bottle of my famous Venom,' said he. 'But take great care of it. You had better give it to Grey Rabbit to put in the medicine cupboard, ready for any Dangerous Visitors.'

'But Weasel is dead,' said Hare, taking it gingerly.

'You never know what may happen,' said Toad, wisely, and Hare put it in his pocket, with the slippers, flute and knife.

As Hare waded through the bog he turned round and saw the Toad busily beating the air with the egg-beater, catching the gossamer cobwebs in its wheels and twisting them into a fish-net.

I should never have thought of that,' he said, and he stopped to pick some grey ash twigs for the Rabbits.

It was dusk when he ran across the fields to Bilberry Wood, and a little crescent moon hung in the sky. His heart was as light as his heels, and he raced along singing:

'Are you there, Mr Moon? Are you there?

Have a care, Mr Moon, here's a Hare.

Columbus, Mr Moon, so Beware——'

'Hello!' said a voice. 'You've been a long time. I have been waiting for hours,' and Hare saw the red-coated gentleman sitting on a stile. At the same moment a strange odour came floating to him, and a dim memory awoke of stories he had heard round the fire at a little house so far away. His heart fluttered and bumped against his side.

'Oh! Sir!' said he, 'you quite startled me. I had forgotten about you.'

'Why, young fellow, I've been expecting you to supper,' replied the Fox with a leer.

'I'm afraid it's too late, I haven't time, thank you. I'll put off my visit, if you don't mind,' said the Hare.

'It's quite early, and really you *must* come, everything is ready, even the red-currant jelly,' and the Fox took his arm and led him down a footpath, between the bilberry clumps, deeper and darker as they scrambled over great rocks and through patches of briar.

It was no use to resist, and Hare pretended not to be afraid. The Fox talked cheerfully all the way, but kept a tight hold of Hare's arm.

Perhaps there was nothing to fear after all.
'I've got a flute,' said Hare, 'I'll show it to you if you let go my arm.' He made one more effort to get away.

'Show it to me in the house,' replied the Fox, 'and then you can play on it,' and he gave Hare's arm a pinch.

They arrived at a ruined Mill house beside a stream. The Fox opened the door and pushed Hare into the kitchen. It really wasn't a gentleman's house, for ragged cobwebs of curtains hung at the windows, and feathers lay piled on the floor. The room had not been dusted for years. Fox was an untidy animal. In a corner lay a gun, a trap, several snares, a jemmy for forcing doors, and a complete burglar's outfit, including handcuffs.

Hare sat uneasily on the edge of a stool, and Fox lay back on a broken rocking-chair.

On the table was a very large dish, as big as Hare, a plate, a long cruel knife and sharp fork, and a pot of red-currant jelly.

'Do you know anything about jugging?' asked Fox, but Hare had never heard of it, and he shook his head.

'It's a new dish, very delicious with jelly,' returned the Fox, dreamily, and he slowly licked his lips.

Hare felt more and more uncomfortable. 'I really must go,' said he, as the stars blinked at him through the broken window, and a little wind moaned round the house. Was Grey Rabbit sitting up for him? Would the Squirrel miss him?

'Not yet, not yet. You've only just come, and I've had no company lately,' said the Fox.

'Would you mind taking off your coat and weskit? They might fit a young friend of mine.'

Hare got more and more alarmed. He handed his lovely blue coat and waistcoat to the Fox, and a paper fell out of the pocket.

'Hello, what's this?' asked the Fox, as he put Hare's watch round his neck, and opened the paper covered with noughts and crosses.

'It's a game,' stammered Hare, 'it's the things I collect.'

'Let us play,' said the Fox, and he drew his chair up to Hare's stool, so that his paws touched Hare's.

'Oh, no, I don't feel well,' faltered Hare.

'Dinner will soon put you right,' and the Fox leaned back and laughed and laughed at Hare's sad face.

So Hare taught noughts and crosses to the Fox, and each game he thought was the last he would play. Fox learned quickly and beat him every time. Hare was too frightened to look what he was doing; his eyes were glancing round the room to find a way of escape. The door was locked, and the broken window gave the only chance.

'That's enough,' said the Fox, putting the pencil and paper in his pocket, and he picked up the coat and turned out the pockets. He brought out the silk handkerchief, and the bundle of ash twigs, a boot-lace, the little slippers, a marble, the flute, and the bottle of Venom.

'Hello? What have we here?' said he, examining the small green bottle. 'Scent? What? Scent? Conceited Hare to carry scent in your pocket!'

He took out the cork and poured some of the liquid on the silk handkerchief. Then he put it to his nose. His eyes closed, his ears drooped, and he sank with his head on the table, insensible.

Hare sprang up, seized the half-empty bottle of Venom, cut the watch from the Fox's neck with his new knife, swept up the slippers, the flute and the ash twigs in his paw, and made for the window. He scrambled through, without waiting for his coat and stick, for already the Fox's eyes were rolling, and his legs kicking.

Away he ran through the wood, tumbling over stones, pitching into brambles, slipping, sliding, rolling down the slopes, his breath panting, his eyes starting.

At first he had no idea where he was, but a glance at the stars showed him the way. He crossed the railway line, and ran through the edge of the village, where dim lights shone in the windows.

When he arrived at the spring he found four sleepy little Rabbits, and a Hedgehog, waiting for him.

'Here he comes, here he comes. Here is Columbus Hare. Hurrah!' they cried. 'What time is it? We've waited for ages.'

'Half-past twelve,' panted Hare, and he stopped a moment to breathe.

'You've been a long time exploring,' said the Hedgehog.

'I stopped to play noughts and crosses with Mr Fox,' said Hare, and they all opened wide their mouths with astonishment.

I didn't forget your ashen twigs,' he continued, giving them the bundle. Then he hurried on without waiting for thanks, up the steep field to the wood.

Each little animal took his twig with the tiny black horse-shoes for luck and nailed it over his door.

'It's been wonderful to meet a real explorer,' they said.

Hare clasped the bottle of Venom tightly in his paw as he went through the deep wood, ready for any Weasel or Stoat whom he might meet, but nobody was abroad. As he ran out of the trees he saw a candle burning in the window of the little house, and he shouted for joy.

Grey Rabbit and Squirrel heard him, and came running down the garden path.

'Oh, Hare, we thought you were dead, especially as Wise Owl told us there was a Fox in Bilberry Wood,' they cried, as they clung to him.

'He caught me,' confessed Hare, 'and I only escaped through Toad's kind present to us all.' He gave a shiver as he thought of the Bilberry Wood and smiling Mr Fox. They entered the house and Hare told his story, and put his presents on the table.

Squirrel tootled on the flute, and little Grey Rabbit tried on the silver birch slippers, which fitted her as if they had been made for her small feet. The Venom she locked up in the medicine cupboard, among the stores of camomile, wormwood, and rue.

'I've had my great adventure,' said Hare. 'I am famous all over the world, and now I shall lead a quiet life at the fire-side.' He wound up his watch, took his lighted candle, and went slowly upstairs to bed.

Grey Rabbit and Squirrel looked at one another and laughed softly. Then they followed, and soon the only sounds in the house by the wood were the snores of Columbus Hare.